WITCH FOR HIRE

WITCH FOR HIRE

TED NAIFEH

AMULET BOOKS • NEW YORK

Library of Congress Control Number: 2020952012

Hardcover ISBN 978-1-4197-4810-3
Paperback ISBN 978-1-4197-4811-0

Book design by Kay Petronio

Published in 2021 by Amulet Books, an imprint of ABRAMS.

Printed and bound in China
10 9 8 7 6 5 4 3 2 1

ABRAMS The Art of Books
195 Broadway, New York, NY 10007
abramsbooks.com

For Charlotte, whose
guidance and
support have been
a revelation.

<

shy_shelbi

3k post 2,3 mil followers 5 following

Do you dream of changing your life? Me too. I tried it all: fitness, fashion, universal one-ness through yoga and healthy bowels . . . but I realized I needed to #transform who I was on the inside. If you want to do what I did, leave weakness behind and become your best self, I can help. Message me up now! I respond to EVERYONE.

Check out my before-and-after photos! It's easier than you think to shed your worries, fears, regrets, and become stronger than you ever dreamed. Meet people just like you who #selfactualized through the shy_shelbi 5-step program.

shy_shelbi
3k post
2,3 mil followers
5 following
Do you dream of changing your life? Me too. I tried it all, fitness, fashion, universal one-ness through yoga and healthy bowels . . . but I realized I needed to #transform who I was on the inside. If you want to do what I did, leave your weakness behind and become your best self, I can help. DM me up now! I respond to EVERYONE.
Follow
Message
Email
5-step program
rules
prizes & penalties
more
Insta-Chat
Dad
Daria
shy_shelbi
Raleigh
Aiden O.
Drucilla
MacKenzie
ting-a-ling

the shy_shelbi program

Step 1: I'm not here to make friends

The world will constantly tell you how much you need people's approval. Don't listen. You don't want to need them, you want them to need you. So step 1 is learning to dominate your social group . . . more

It's kinda like wading into icy water . . .
SO MACKENZIE DID FOUR PHOTOSHOOTS OVER THE SUMMER. GUESS HER SO-CALLED MODELING CAREER IS REAL AFTER ALL.
YEAH, I HEARD. KNOW WHAT SHE'S SAYING ABOUT IT?

Every inch you sink is agony. Knowing there's more to come makes it worse.
"IT'S NO BIG DEAL."
ugh!
SHE'S LITERALLY THE WORST.
umm, HEY, BRYCE? CAN I, uh . . .

WHAT DO YOU THINK YOU'RE **DOING**, CODY?
I JUST THOUGHT—
YOU THOUGHT BECAUSE I'M YOUR **SISTER**, I'M GONNA **BABYSIT** YOU?
THIS IS YOUR ***SISTER?***

OH YEAH, I SEE THE **RESEMBLANCE**. YOU COULD BE **TWINS**.
REALLY, DREW?
HOW'S THAT MOUTH-BREATHING **ZIT-FACTORY** YOU CALL A **BROTHER?** STILL LIVING IN YOUR MOM'S ***GARAGE?***
WHAT IS HE NOW, ***23?***

OH, YOU ***REALLY*** WANNA GO THERE? AT LEAST ***MY*** MOM'S NEVER BEEN IN A ***MENTAL HOSPITAL***.

DUDE, YOUR MOM'S IN A MENTAL— ?
ARE YOU TALKING, DARIA!?
YOUR SHADOW IS STILL HERE.

Oh, FOR CHRIST'S— GET LOST, CODY!
BUT . . .
THE ONLY OTHER SEAT IS AT THE . . .

. . . LOSER TABLE.

WELL, AT LEAST YOU KNOW WHERE YOU **STAND**.
It's only when you just dive in, get it over with, you realize, after the horrible shock . . .
DON'T WORRY, SIS.
YOU'LL FIT RIGHT IN.
. . . it's not so bad. You can live with this.
uh . . . IS THIS SEAT, uh . . .

SURE, PLEASE JOIN US.
KILL YOURSELF LOSER
It's amazing what you can learn to live with.

ON ONE CONDITION.
TRY ONE OF THESE. MY SPECIAL RECIPE.
WHAT . . . WHAT'S IN 'EM?
WHO KNOWS? COULD BE ANYTHING. EYE OF NEWT, TOE OF FROG . . .

WOOL OF BAT, AND TONGUE OF DOG!
ADDER'S FORK, AND BLIND-WORM'S STING . . .

OR MORE LIKELY JUST A LITTLE ORANGE ZEST.

RELAX, DEARIE. HAVE A SEAT.

AND JÚLIO, THAT'S PROBABLY ENOUGH SHAKESPEARE FOR ONE DAY.
HOW DARE YOU?! THERE'S NO SUCH THING AS ENOUGH SHAKESPEARE.
LOSER

THIS IS AMAZING!

ORANGE ZEST. THE MAGIC INGREDIENT.
SEE? THE LOSER TABLE HAS ITS PERKS.

LEMME GUESS. SOMEONE TOLD YOU IF YOU ENDED UP HERE YOU'D BE A LOSER FOR LIFE.
MY BIG SISTER, BRYCE. SHE SAYS IT'S CURSED.

EXCEPT ANTOINE LEVIN USED TO SIT HERE. THEN, HE GREW TWO FEET OVERNIGHT. NOW HE'S THE STAR PLAYER ON THE VARSITY TEAM.
TOINE? YOU MEAN THE GUY DATING MACKENZIE MERCADO?
I HEARD SHE'S ALREADY MODELING FOR MAGAZINES.

OH YEAH, MACKENZIE.
HER FIRST DAY? HEADGEAR, SWOLLEN GUMS, FRIZZY HAIR, THE WORKS. STRAIGHT TO THE LOSER TABLE.
WHERE DO YOU THINK SHE AND TOINE MET?
MILK

RIGHT WHERE YOU'RE SITTING.
NO WAY!

RAFFI IS ONLY STUCK HERE TILL EVERYONE FIGURES OUT HE LIVES IN A MANSION WITH AN OLYMPIC SWIMMING POOL. THEN HE'S DOOMED.
AND JIYOUNG IS GOING TO A GIFTED SCHOOL WITH ACTUAL WHEELCHAIR ACCESSIBILITY.
YOU'RE ABOUT THE ONLY THING I'LL MISS ABOUT THIS DUMP, FAYE.

AND OBVIOUSLY, JÚLIO WILL BE IN THE DRAMA CLUB BY NEXT WEEK.
HAH!!!
KURT LASKY AND THOSE DOLTS STAGING RENT LIKE IT'S STILL A THING?
I THINK NOT!

WHAT ABOUT **YOU?** WHEN ARE **YOU** MOVING ON?
ME? I'M THE ONLY **PERMANENT RESIDENT.**
MILK

HOW **COME?** YOU'RE PRETTY **NORMAL**. I MEAN, OTHER THAN . . .
uh . . .
YOU MEAN MY TOTALLY RANK **STYLE?**
errr . . .

WELCOME TO THE ***LOSER TABLE,*** KIDDO. BETTER GET ***USED*** TO IT.
MILK

ANOTHER GOOD THING ABOUT THE LOSER TABLE, NO ONE PRETENDS TO LIKE YOU. THERE'S NOTHING IN IT FOR 'EM.
THAT'S A GOOD THING?
HERE SHE COMES.
I DON'T KNOW, BUT IT'S HILARIOUS.
WHO DID THAT?
shhhh!

OH MY GOD! WHAT HAPPENED?
AREN'T YOU UPSET?
BEATS ME.
PEOPLE PULL PRANKS LIKE THIS ALL THE TIME.
IF I LET IT STRESS ME OUT, THEY WIN.
SATAN'S LITTLE HELPER

BESIDES, NOW MY LOCKER IS EASIER TO FIND.

YOU REALLY DON'T CARE WHAT PEOPLE THINK OF YOU?
SHOULD I? WHAT'S IN IT FOR ME?

BRYCE? CODY? DINNERTIME!
OH BOO-HOO! HIS HOUSE GOT BURIED IN A LANDSLIDE. HOW IS THIS MY FAULT?
AND WITH ALEXA GONE AND MACKENZIE TOO BUSY WITH HER OH-SO-IMPORTANT MODELING CAREER, I'M A LOCK FOR DEBATE TEAM CAPTAIN.
THE ONUS IS ON HIM. HE SHOULD HAVE BROUGHT IN A PROPER BUILDING INSPECTOR.
FIRST THING I LEARNED IN REAL ESTATE. WANT SOMETHING DONE RIGHT? HIRE AN EXPERT.

DAD! DEBATE TEAM CAPTAIN!
rmmm.
COOL, RIGHT? AND AIDEN OLRICH IS GONNA ASK ME OUT. YOU REMEMBER, HIS DAD IS THE CEO OF-
TELL HIM TO GET LOST.

T— TELL HIM—?
IF HE THINKS HE CAN PROVE **LIABILITY,** HE CAN TRY **SUING** US AND SEE WHERE IT **GETS** HIM.
BUT HE MAY WANT TO SPRING FOR AN **ACTUAL LAWYER.**

AND HOW WAS **YOUR** FIRST DAY, HONEYBUN? DID YOU MAKE ANY NEW **FRIENDS?**
uh, **YEAH,** ACTUALLY.

I MEAN, THEY'RE NOT THE **COOLEST** KIDS IN SCHOOL, BUT THEY'RE, YA KNOW, **NICE** . . .
WELL, **I** THINK **COOL** IS A LITTLE OVERRATED **ANYWAY**.
heh, **YEAH**. THERE'S THIS **ONE** GIRL, THOUGH . . .
A **COOL** GIRL?

SHE'S KINDA TOO **COOL** TO BE COOL . . .
IF **THAT** MAKES SENSE.

OH **RIGHT,** CODY'S NEW **BESTIE.**
TELL US ALL ABOUT **FAYE FAULKNER,** CODY. DID SHE TELL YOU WHY SHE **DRESSES** LIKE THAT?

IS SHE, LIKE, A **DEVIL WORSHIPPER?**
OR DOES SHE HAVE **EMOTIONAL PROBLEMS?**
ooh! **MAYBE** SHE HAS NO IDEA SHE'S **DOING** IT. **CRAY**-CRAAAAY . . .

DRESSES LIKE **WHAT,** HON?
SHE'S JUST—
CODY!

I FORBID YOU TO BE FRIENDS WITH THAT GIRL.
THAT FAULKNER GIRL IS A TROUBLE-MAKER.
W-WHAT? WHY?

HOWARD, CODY HAS A TOUGH TIME MAKING FRIENDS. MAYBE WE—
I'M GONNA STOP YOU RIGHT THERE.
THIS GIRL STIRRED UP A SCANDAL IN HER HOMETOWN, AND CAME HERE TO GET AWAY FROM IT.

IT WAS ALL OVER THE NEWS, REMEMBER? TWO YEARS AGO.
I . . . MAYBE?

YOUR ACTIONS REFLECT ON THIS FAMILY, YOUNG LADY.
I CAN'T HAVE MY DAUGHTER HANGING AROUND WITH A JUVENILE DELINQUENT.
IT LOOKS BAD. ESPECIALLY AFTER YOUR MOTHER'S . . . TROUBLES.

YES, BUT . . .
MAYBE CODY COULD JUST TRY TO BE A GOOD INFLUENCE ON THIS GIRL. MY THERAPIST SAYS THAT—

ARE YOU KIDDING ME?!
YOU ARE THE LAST PERSON WHO SHOULD BE GIVING OUT PERSONAL ADVICE!

YOU HAVE NO IDEA WHAT AN EMBARRASSMENT YOU ARE, DO YOU?! EVERYONE KNOWS ABOUT YOU! IT'S HUMILIATING!
CAN YOU PLEASE NOT SCREW UP THIS FAMILY EVEN WORSE THAN YOU ALREADY HAVE?

S-SORRY, DAD. SORRY, BRYCE.

I'LL . . .
I'LL TRY TO DO BETTER.

YES, AS A MATTER OF FACT, I DO WEAR MY HAT EVERY DAY.

WHAT'S YOUR POINT?
JUST THAT IF YOU DRESSED, YOU KNOW, NORMALLY . . .

BUT I DON'T.
YEAH, BUT . . .

I'M JUST SAYING YOU'RE COOL, OKAY?
AND THE ONLY REASON YOU'RE STILL STUCK HERE AFTER TWO YEARS . . .
GOSH, THANKS.

STUCK WHERE? AT THE LOSER TABLE?
...IS BECAUSE OF THAT SILLY HAT!
OKAY?
SO?

SO... IF YOU LOSE THE HAT, YOU WON'T BE STUCK AT THE LOSER TABLE ANYMORE.
IT'S JUST A HAT, RIGHT? WHAT'S THE BIG DEAL?

I DON'T KNOW. ASK THEM. THEY'RE THE ONES WHO CAN'T BE FRIENDS WITH SOMEONE BECAUSE OF A SILLY HAT.

BUT MY POINT IS—
YOUR POINT IS I SHOULD STOP LOOKING LIKE I WANT, AND LOOK LIKE THEY WANT. AND THEN THEY'LL BE MY FRIENDS. EXCEPT I DON'T CALL THAT FRIENDSHIP.

CAN YOU BLAME THEM? YOU'RE WEARING A HALLOWEEN COSTUME!
IT'S . . . WEIRD!

SO WHAT? IT'S NOT HURTING ANYONE. IT'S NOT A NAZI UNIFORM.
THAT'S NOT WHAT I—
MILK

AND IT'S NOT A COSTUME. IT'S WHO I AM. AND IF YOU THINK I SHOULD GIVE THAT UP TO MAKE FRIENDS . . .

. . . THEN YOU AND I HAVE A VERY DIFFERENT IDEA OF WHAT FRIENDSHIP IS!

I GUESS I'LL SIT SOMEWHERE **ELSE** THEN.
YOU **DO** THAT.

DAMN, FAYE. AND YOU CALL **ME** DRAMATIC.

SOB
ARE YOU OKAY IN THERE? SOMETHING WRONG?

WHAT . . . ? OH, NOTHING, JUST . . .

EVERYONE HATES ME, AND I'VE GOT NO FRIENDS.
I SEE.

WHAT IF I TOLD YOU I KNOW A WAY TO CHANGE ALL THAT?

SATANS LITTLE HELPER

SATANS LITTLE HELPER

FIGHTIN SPIRIT!
sigh

shy__shelbi
3k post
2,3 mil followers
5 following
Follow
Message
Email
5-step program
rules
prizes & penalties
more
insta-chat
Shy__Shelbi
SS
The rules are so simple. Any idiot could follow them. Maybe you don't have what it takes.
This is your last chance. Don't fail again.
You'll need 6 cans of spray paint. Go to the south parking lot. No one will be there. Await my instructions.

the shy_shelbi program

Step 2: Sounds like a "you" problem

People often think that because they have an issue, it's everyone's issue. Don't let them weigh you down with their emotional baggage. Step 2, detachment . . . more

YOU REALLY THINK FAULKNER DID THIS? I KNOW SHE'S UNSTABLE, BUT . . .
IT'S GOTTA BE HER. SHE'S ANGRY ABOUT HER LOCKER. THOUGHT SHE'D TAKE IT OUT ON EVERYONE.
I THOUGHT YOU SAID SHE DID THAT HERSELF FOR ATTENTION.
21

ARE YOU TALKING, DARIA?!
uh, NO.

STUFF LIKE THIS IS ALWAYS THE CREEPY LITTLE OUTSIDER TRYING TO GET EVEN. TRUST ME.

ONE MORE WEEK, JIYOUNG. STAY STRONG.
One by one, they all move on, saying we'll stay friends, never really meaning it.
YOU TOO, FAYE.

It's fine, though. I've learned not to get attached. Being alone is one thing I know how to handle.
HEY, FAYE?

oh, CODY. WHAT DO YOU WANT?
uh . . .
I, uh . . .
MY BIG SISTER THINKS YOU DID THE . . . "BUTTS" THING.

I THINK THEY'RE GONNA . . .
YEAH. THEY'RE ALREADY HERE.

THINK IT'S FUNNY SPRAY PAINTING MY LEXUS?
sigh
BECAUSE OF COURSE YOU THINK IT WAS ME.

I'M SORRY! I TRIED TO WARN YOU—
WE KNOW IT WAS YOU, YOU LITTLE FREAK!
WHO ELSE WOULD IT BE?
WELL, I GUESS THAT DECIDES IT. MY MOM TAUGHT ME NEVER TO ARGUE WITH LOGIC.
OR IDIOTS.
WHERE DO YOU THINK YOU'RE—

—GOING . . .
WHAT THE HELL?

OVER THERE!

HOW'D SHE GET ALL THE WAY—

ACTUALLY, I'M OVER HERE.
WAIT! MAYBE I'M HERE!

WHAT'S GOING ON?
DO YOU SEE HER?
SHE'S HERE SOMEWHERE.

WHERE ARE YOU, YOU LITTLE—

WITCH?

I'LL KILL—
OW!

SHE WAS RIGHT THERE!
WHERE IS SHE NOW?
OVER THERE! GET HER!

OH-pp!

THAT OUGHT TO GET RID OF 'EM.
HOW . . . ? HOW!?

HOW
WHAT?
YOU WERE
IN TWO PLACES
AT ONCE.

I
SAW
YOU.
I
TOLD
YOU.

IT'S
NOT A
COSTUME.

WAIT,
WHAT?

HANG ON A MINUTE. WHAT ARE YOU SAYING?
SO YOU, LIKE, HAVE MAGICAL POWERS?
WHAT ELSE CAN YOU DO?
NONE OF YOUR BUSINESS.
ARE YOU SERIOUS?
YOU CAN'T JUST DROP A BOMBSHELL LIKE THAT AND THEN WALK AWAY LIKE IT'S NOTHING.
PRETTY SURE I'M ABOUT TO, DEARIE.
WELL, WHAT'S TO STOP ME FROM TELLING EVERYONE?

TELL THEM I'M A **REAL WITCH** WITH **MAGICAL POWERS?**
HOW DO YOU THINK ***THAT'LL*** PLAY OUT?
DO YOURSELF A **FAVOR.** GO **HOME,** AND PRETEND NONE OF THIS EVER **HAPPENED.**
FAYE, IT . . .
IT WAS ***ME!***

huh?

THE **CARS.** THE ***BUTTS.*** IT WAS **ME.**
WHY?
AND WHY ARE YOU ***TELLING*** ME?

BECAUSE . . . NO ONE ELSE WOULD ***BELIEVE*** ME.

WHEN I FIRST SAW HER **PROFILE,** I THOUGHT IT WAS A ***JOKE.***
BUT THE **MESSAGES** KEPT **COMING,** SAYING SOMETHING **TERRIBLE** WOULD HAPPEN IF I DIDN'T FOLLOW THE RULES.
I **IGNORED** THEM. TWO DAYS LATER, MY **MOM** HAD HER **CAR ACCIDENT.**
SOMEONE CUT THE . . .
err . . . WHAT'S-IT? **BRAKE LINE.** ON HER **MINIVAN.**

SHE WENT OVER A TEN-FOOT **DROP.**
ATION
CAUTION
CAUTION
CAUTI
CAUTION
AUTION

SHE'S STILL IN THE **ICU.** SHE LOOKS . . . ***HORRIBLE.***

CAN'T BELIEVE I'M ASKING, BUT DID YOU TRY CALLING THE POLICE.

THEY'RE STUCK. THE VAN WAS LOCKED IN THE GARAGE. NO ONE COULD HAVE GOTTEN IN.
huh. AND THIS SHABBY SHARON? WHAT DID SHE LOOK LIKE?

SHY SHELBI. I NEVER SAW HER FACE. SHE JUST TOLD ME TO MESSAGE HER.
AND YOU HAVEN'T TALKED TO HER SINCE THE FIRST DAY?
JUST THROUGH INSTA-CHAT. BUT . . .
WOMAN

I FEEL LIKE SHE'S WATCHING ME.
ALL THE TIME.

WHY ARE YOU TELLING ME ALL THIS?
I THOUGHT MAYBE, LIKE, YA KNOW . . . YOU COULD USE YOUR POWERS?

MY POWERS?
YOUR WITCHCRAFT. TO HELP ME.

MY DAD SAYS IF YOU CAN'T DO SOMETHING YOURSELF, HIRE AN EXPERT. HE'S KIND OF A BIG DEAL, AND . . .
UM . . . MAYBE HE COULD PAY YOU?

SORRY. I'M NOT THAT KIND OF WITCH.
WHAT KIND?
FOR HIRE.

WELL, err . . . DO YOU, LIKE, KNOW ONE?
A WITCH FOR HIRE?
ANYONE WHO COULD HELP ME!

sigh
I DID ONCE. THE WITCH WHO TAUGHT ME EVERYTHING I KNOW.
OL' LADY LEDOUX, THEY CALLED HER.
SHE ALWAYS HELPED. IF THERE WAS A CURSE TO BREAK, A HAUNTING TO SORT OUT. EVEN JUST WHEN SOME JERK WAS BEATING UP HIS KIDS.

SHE WASN'T AFRAID OF ANYTHING OR ANYONE. NOT MONSTERS, HUMAN OR OTHERWISE.
NOT PARENTS' GROUPS, OR ANGRY MOBS, OR CITY HALL. NOBODY.

I'M SURE YOU CAN GUESS HOW THAT WORKED OUT.
I GUESS SHE WASN'T TOO POPULAR.

YEAH, YOU COULD SAY THAT. EVENTUALLY, SOMEONE KILLED HER.

OH MY GOD! DID THEY CATCH WHOEVER DID IT?

"THEY"? WHO WOULD "THEY" CATCH? THEMSELVES?

THEY DON'T EVEN PRETEND TO DO THAT ANYMORE. THERE WAS AN "INQUIRY," BUT IT WAS A JOKE. THE GUY BASICALLY JUST WALKED AWAY.

AND ALL THE PEOPLE SHE STOOD UP FOR AND HELPED OVER THE YEARS?
NOT A SINGLE ONE CAME FORWARD TO DEFEND HER NAME.
ONLY ME.

AND JUST LIKE THAT, I LOST ALL MY FRIENDS.

SO YOU'LL UNDERSTAND IF I DON'T STICK MY NOSE IN OTHER PEOPLE'S BUSINESS.
THE LAST LESSON I LEARNED FROM MY TEACHER?
IT'S NOT WORTH IT.

SO THAT'S IT? AWFUL THINGS HAPPEN TO INNOCENT PEOPLE, AND THERE'S NOTHING YOU CAN DO ABOUT IT? YOU HURT OTHERS OR YOU GET HURT?

THAT'S JUST HOW THE WORLD WORKS, DEARIE. BETTER GET USED TO IT.

MONKEY'S PAW CURSES OVER THE INTERNET. GUESS IT WAS INEVITABLE.

JUST CHECK THE RECIPE, WOULD YOU, DEARIE? IT'S UNDER C FOR "CRISP."
YIKES! WHO'S THIS CREEPER?

OH, HIM. THAT'S WHAT I CALL A "CURSE CREATURE." THAT ONE WAS A REAL CHARMER.
WAIT, THIS IS A REAL THING?

NOT EXACTLY. CURSE CREATURES EXIST SOMEWHERE BETWEEN THE REAL WORLD AND THE REALM OF IDEAS, I GUESS YOU COULD SAY.

WHAT DOES THAT MEAN? DOES IT EXIST OR DOESN'T IT?
EXACTLY.

ARE YOU MAKING FUN OF ME?
THINGS AIN'T ALWAYS ONE THING OR THE OTHER. THEY CAN BE IN BETWEEN.
PPER
SALT

CURSES CAN BE LIKE THAT, NEITHER REAL NOR UNREAL. YOU CAN'T NEVER PROVE THEY MAKE THINGS HAPPEN.
BUT YOU CAN'T DENY 'EM NEITHER, 'CAUSE THINGS KEEP HAPPENIN' WHETHER YOU BELIEVE IT OR NOT.
PELT
FLOUR
SU

REMEMBER THE **MONKEY'S PAW** CURSE?

A MONKEY PUTS ITS HAND IN A **HOLE** TO GET THE **TREAT** INSIDE. BUT WHEN IT CLOSES ITS **FIST,** IT CAN'T PULL IT **OUT**.
FLOUR

NOW IT'S **TRAPPED,** 'CAUSE IT CAN'T BRING ITSELF TO **LET GO** OF THE TREAT.

SO, THE **CURSE** IS **THREE WISHES** THAT ALWAYS GO **WRONG**.
Monkey's Paw
BUT THE VICTIM CAN'T NEVER **ABANDON** THE WISHES, 'CAUSE THEY CAN'T RESIST HOPING THE **NEXT ONE** WILL GIVE 'EM THEIR HEART'S **DESIRE.**

NUTMEG
CINNAMON
THAT WAS **THIS** HANDSOME FELLA'S LITTLE GAME. TILL **I** CAME ALONG.
YOU **STOPPED** HIM? **HOW?**

THAT'S A LONG STORY FOR ANOTHER TIME, DEARIE. GET THE DOOR, WILL YOU?
BING BONG

OH, FAYE. WHAT ARE YOU DOING HERE?
BAKING. CAN I HELP YOU, MRS. WILCOX?

FOR HEAVEN'S SAKE, FAYE. CAN'T YOU SEE SHE'S TIRED? YOU BETTER COME IN, ELLEN.
FLOUR

GINGER CAKE? MADE IT JUST THIS MORNING. FAYE LIKES IT WITH ICE CREAM. THINK I STILL GOT SOME IF YOU'RE INTERESTED.
I'M SO SORRY TO BOTHER YOU, ELVIRA.
ARE YOU? WELL, THAT'S A FIRST, I RECKON. WHAT CAN I DO FOR YOU, ELLEN?

I'M . . .
I'M AFRAID TO GO HOME. BUT I'M EVEN MORE AFRAID OF WHAT FRANK MIGHT DO IF I DON'T.
YOU MEAN TO THE CHILDREN?

HE'S NOT A BAD MAN.

WHAT DO YOU WANT ME TO SAY? THAT FRANK IS SORRY? THAT HE WON'T DO IT AGAIN? THAT'S WHAT YOUR FRIENDS ALWAYS SAY, AIN'T IT?

BUT YOU CAME TO ME THIS TIME, BECAUSE YOU WANT THE TRUTH, AND YOU KNEW I'D TELL IT STRAIGHT.

HE'S GONNA KILL YOU, ELLEN. SOONER OR LATER, IF YOU KEEP PUTTIN' YOURSELF BETWEEN HIS FISTS AND YOUR KIDS.
YOU'VE GOTTA GET 'EM OUT OF THERE.

HE WON'T LET ME.
HE WILL IF I'M THERE.

I CAN'T LET HIM HURT YOU TOO.
YOU LET ME WORRY ABOUT THAT. HE'S JUST A BULLY, AND I KNOW HOW TO STAND UP TO BULLIES. BEEN DOIN' IT ALL MY LIFE.

I...
I CAN'T DO THIS. I'M NOT BRAVE ENOUGH. I'M NOT LIKE YOU, ELVIRA. I'VE NEVER STOOD UP TO ANYONE.

YOU'D BE SURPRISED. SOMETIMES, YOU FIND MORE STRENGTH INSIDE YOU THAN YOU EVER THOUGHT YOU HAD.
EAT YOUR CAKE. JUST BETWEEN YOU AND ME, THERE'S A LITTLE MAGIC IN THE GINGER.

MIGHT JUST GIVE YOU THE COURAGE YOU NEED.
ARE YOU MAKING FUN OF ME?
NOT AT ALL.

I THOUGHT YOU HATED MRS. WILCOX.
SURE DO. SHE'S BEEN TRYING TO RUN ME OUT OF TOWN FOR TWENTY YEARS.
SO WHY ARE YOU HELPING HER?

AIN'T YOU LEARNED NOTHING?
ELLEN NEEDS HELP, AND AIN'T NO ONE ELSE GONNA HELP HER. IF I DON'T NEITHER, I'M AS GOOD AS LETTING HER DIE.

MAYBE SOME FOLKS COULD LIVE WITH THAT, BUT NOT ME.
BUT YOU SAID IT YOURSELF! MR. WILCOX IS OUT OF CONTROL. HE'LL HURT YOU!

NOT IF I GOT THIS.
WHAT IS THAT?
CALL IT A LUCKY CHARM.

ELVIRA?
I'M READY. YOU SURE YOU WANT TO DO THIS?

WOULDN'T MISS IT FOR THE WORLD, DEARIE. LET'S GET THEM KIDS SAFE.

HEY GRETCHEN. WANT IN?

DON'T JUDGE ME. WHAT DO YOU KNOW? YOU'RE JUST A CAT!

FINE!
OKAY, SHY SHELBI. LET'S DANCE.

the shy_shelbi program

Step 3: Don't @ Me

No one will thank you for living your best life. They'll act like your #selfactualization is somehow hurting them. Before you take on other people's interpretation of reality, ask yourself, how right could it be if it just makes their life suck? Step 3, defending your reality . . . more

DUDE! SOMEONE SET THE PLAYGROUND AT NEWBURY PARK ON FIRE LAST NIGHT.

HOMECOMING DANCE

- Faye's Journal, October 3rd -

Elvira said things like curse creatures exist in "the Ethereal," a space between the real and the unreal.

I HEARD. SICK! HEAR ABOUT THE RAT POISON THEY FOUND IN CEREAL BOXES AT THE GROCERY STORE?

THANKS FOR JOINING US, BOYS. AS I WAS SAYING . . .

I HEARD IT WAS CAT FOOD. THAT'S MESSED UP!

SODIUM.

This makes them hard to fight.

IN ITS PURE FORM, HIGHLY VOLATILE. ADD HYDROXIDE, IT BECOMES LYE. MORE STABLE, THOUGH STILL QUITE CAUSTIC WHEN IT COMES IN CONTACT WITH WATER. BUT . . .

. . . MIXED WITH CHLORIDE, IT BECOMES ORDINARY TABLE SALT, COMPLETELY—

FOOOOOOM
So you start by studying their movements. Their modus operandi.
ARE YOU ALL RIGHT, MR. KAUFMAN?
IS THE SCHOOL GONNA BURN DOWN?

PLEASE EXIT THE CLASSROOM IN AN ORDERLY FASHION, PEOPLE.
BRO! THAT WAS SICK!
BEST FIFTH PERIOD EVER, YO!
YEAH SCIENCE!

INTERESTING.
MORE ORDERLY THAN THAT, MISS FAULKNER.
Sooner or later, a pattern will emerge.

MISS FAULKNER?
HELLO?

- Faye's Journal, October 5th -
Pranks need an audience. The bigger the better.
LADIES AND GENTLEMEN, ALLOW ME TO INTRODUCE THIS YEAR'S HOMECOMING KING AND QUEEN . . .

So I had a hunch Homecoming would be Shy Shelbi's ideal hunting ground.
ANTOINE LEVIN AND MACKENZIE MERCADO!
LET'S GIVE THEM A WARM DANVILLE HIGH WELCOME HOME.
QUEEN
AND NOW, THE HOMECOMING KING AND QUEEN WILL LEAD THE FIRST . . .
WHAT THE—!?
WHOA, IS THAT . . . AIDEN OLRICH?
IT TOTALLY IS!

DUDE, EVERYONE KNOWS ABOUT KURT LASKY THERE, BUT—

HA HA! WHO KNEW OLRICH WAS A THEATER LOVER?
I, uh, LISTEN, BRYCE, I WAS JUST MESSING—
EXIT

OOF!!!
WHAK
WHOA!

YOU'RE STILL DEAD MEAT, FREAK! YOU CAN'T PLAY HIDE-AND-SEEK FOREVER.
GREAT. GLAD WE HAD THIS TALK, BRYCE.
HOMECOMING DANCE
YAZ QUEEN
Turns out I was right. And once you can predict your target's behavior ...

oh, HEY CODY. THAT WAS SOME MESS, huh? I HOPE KURT AND AIDEN ARE OKAY—
I, uh . . .
I GOT ANOTHER MESSAGE.
It's just a matter of laying the right trap.

AND?
IT SAID I GOTTA . . .
. . . PUSH YOU DOWN THE STAIRS.

PRETEND IT WAS AN ACCIDENT.
YEAH, I FIGURED IT'D BE SOMETHING LIKE THAT.

wh-WHAT?!
AFTER YOU LEFT THE OTHER NIGHT, I MESSAGED SHELBI. GOT MY FIRST CHALLENGE.

THAT'S CRAZY! WHY?
I WANTED TO SEE WHAT WOULD HAPPEN IF I TOLD SHY SHELBI WHERE TO STICK HER LITTLE GAME.
AND NOW I KNOW. SHE SENT YOU.
BUT IF I DON'T . . .

SO DO IT.
WHAT? I CAN'T JUST—

DO IT NOW!

AAAAHH!

OH MY GOD!
WHAT THE HELL!

YOU PUSHED HER!!! WHAT ARE YOU, CRAZY?
I DIDN'T . . .
I DIDN'T MEAN—
I SAW IT TOO! SHE JUST—
HEY, SHELBI!

BOO!

SKRRREEEEEEEEEE

AAAAAGH!!!

WHAT WAS THAT?
IS SHE OKAY DOWN HERE?

CAN YOU MOVE? HOW MANY FINGERS AM I HOLDING UP?
I'M NOT TAKING MATH ASSIGNMENTS FROM YOU, GLENN.

YOU SHOULDN'T STAND UP. YOU MIGHT HAVE AMNESIA!
THAT'S THE KID THAT DID IT. SHE TOTALLY PUSHED YOU—
ARE YOU OKAY?
OW!
I'M AWESOME.

I GOT THIS SHELBI CHARACTER RIGHT WHERE I WANT HER.

SOMEONE DID WHAT!? THAT'S NOT A PRANK, THAT'S A HATE CRIME!
WE'RE GOING TO SPEAK TO PRINCIPAL ATLEY RIGHT NOW!
CAN WE JUST GO HOME PLEASE? I WANT TO GO HOME!
ARE YOU SURE YOU'RE OKAY?

YEAH. I HAVE A MAGIC WARD TO PROTECT ME FROM STUFF LIKE THAT.

SEE?
BUT . . . YOUR ARM!

THIS? IT'S A BIT LIKE A PSYCHIC WOUND. GUESS MY WARD DOESN'T WORK FOR THAT.
THAT'S THE RISK OF CROSSING BACK AND FORTH, ESPECIALLY WITHOUT A CIRCLE OF PROTECTION.
YOU CAN TAKE STUFF WITH YOU.
IT LOOKS PRETTY PHYSICAL TO ME.

LIKE MOST CURSE CREATURES, SHY SHELBI ONLY EXISTS IN THE SPIRIT WORLD.
SHE DOESN'T HURT PEOPLE PHYSICALLY, EXCEPT THROUGH OTHERS, LIKE YOU.

BUT WITH THIS, I THINK I CAN . . .
HEY! ARE YOU EVEN LISTENING TO ME?

OH, I'M SORRY! IS MY BATTLE WITH A SUPERNATURAL ENTITY BORING YOU?

YOU KNOW WHAT? I DON'T NEED THIS! WHY AM I RISKING MY NECK FOR A LITTLE PUNK WHO DOESN'T EVEN—
IS THAT . . . I THINK . . .

JÚLIO?

WAIT!!!

SKREEEEEEEEEEEE

SHE JUST RAN OUT—
THEY CAME OUT OF NOWHERE! I DIDN'T—!
OH LORD!
SHE WAS PUSHING THAT OTHER KID OUT OF THE WAY!
insta-chat
shy_shelbi
Kill yourself, loser.
There ain't no shortage of theories about curse creatures and where they come from.

Druids and shamans thought they were a sign of a society falling out of harmony with the natural world.

Ancient superstition reckoned them the vengeful will of the unquiet dead.

GREAT.
Ancient superstition reckoned them the vengeful will of the unquiet dead. Christians thought it was Satan. Or witches. Of course, everything those folk don't care for gets tarred with the same brush.
Truth is, no one knows what, or who, brings Curse Creatures into the world. Which makes them hard to get rid of.

IN THIS PLACE, I AM IN MY ELEMENT.
IN THIS CIRCLE, I AM IN MY POWER.

WITH THIS WAND, OF, UM, CEDAR? I CONVEY MY WILL UNTO THE WORLD.
WITH THIS . . . BUTTERKNIFE OF SILVER, I CLEAVE LIES FROM TRUTH.
GRETCHEN

THIS CHALICE SHALL REFLECT ONLY TRUTH. SHOW ME . . .

SHOW ME THE FACE OF MY ENEMY.

ting-a-ling
DAMMIT! I TURNED YOU OFF.

GRETCHEN, DID YOU—

KEEP IT TOGETHER, FAYE.
FIRST SIGN OF MADNESS, TALKING TO THE CAT.

CLICK

GAAAH!

ting-a-ling

shy_shelbi
SS
loser.

YEAH? WELL, THIS LOSER GOT A PIECE OF YOU.
ting-a-ling

SS loser.
and I got a piece of you. Yummy.
THINGS LIKE YOU DON'T JUST HAPPEN.

DID SOMEONE SUMMON YOU? I WANT A NAME.
ting-a-ling
You all did. All the losers. You called me. You worshipped me.

"I hate the way I look."
"No one sees the real me."
"No one will ever love me."
"I wish I was dead."
ting-a-ling
Prayers to shy_shelbi, patron saint of losers.

SOMEONE MUST HAVE STARTED IT!
ting-a-ling
Maybe it was you, Faye Faulkner.
THAT'S CRAP! I DON'T HATE MYSELF!
Oh, right! You just hate everyone else.

WHAT ARE YOU TALKING ABOUT?
SS
"I'm the witch girl, the noble pariah. No one is worthy to be my friend. They're all shallow fools."
"But it's better this way. I don't need them. I don't need anyone."
SS
ting-a-ling

SHUT UP!
SNAP

I BIND YOU BY THE NAME SHY SHELBI!

TO THIS VESSEL, I BIND YOU!!!
ting -a- ling

IDIOT GIRL! YOU WOULD LOCK ME IN HERE? THIS IS MY HOME! THIS IS MY HUNTING GROUND!

YOU'RE ALL TRAPPED IN HERE WITH ME!!!
I BANISH YOU!

ting-a-ling

You think I can't touch you? Maybe not. But your little trinket can't protect your friends.

THEY'RE **NOT** MY **FRIENDS.** DO WHAT YOU **LIKE.** I'M **NOT** GONNA PLAY YOUR ***GAME.***
UNWOMAN

But your little trinket can't protect your friends.
SS
And what about your mom?
ting-a-ling

Witch or not, you're going to play my game, Faye Faulkner. Like all the rest.

the shy_shelbi program

Step 4: Too Blessed to be Stressed

Successful people make losers uncomfortable. They will act like there's something wrong with you when you leave them behind in their misery. But you get to decide what matters and what's not worth losing sleep over. Step 4 is turning other people's jealousy to your benefit . . . more

MR. ATLEY?
sigh
MR. SPOONER, TURNING EVERYONE AGAINST THE FACULTY ISN'T GOING TO MAKE THIS GO AWAY.
WHAT DO I CARE ABOUT A FEW PRANKS? I JUST WANTED LEVERAGE OVER THE SCHOOL BOARD.
AND YOU.

WHAT? WHY?
YOU'VE GOT CONNECTIONS AT HARVARD, RIGHT?
MY DAUGHTER BRYCE IS GRADUATING SOON. I NEED TO KNOW YOU'RE AS CONCERNED ABOUT HER FUTURE AS I AM.

Spooner & Associates
Development and Construction
Howard Spooner
MY CARD. I'LL BE EXPECTING YOUR CALL. GOOD LUCK WITH THIS PRANK BUSINESS.

YOU'RE . . . BLACKMAILING ME? WHO THE HELL DO YOU THINK YOU ARE?
I'M A BIG DEAL IN THIS TOWN, ATLEY. AND YOU'LL FIND I MAKE A BETTER FRIEND THAN AN ENEMY.

-Faye's Journal, October 10th -
Ever since Elvira died, solitude has been my safe space. No one could let me down if I didn't care.
Or so I thought. But not anymore.

RAFF! THIS WEEKEND? POOL PARTY?
I'LL HAVE TO ASK MY PARENTS.
JUST SAYIN'.

SEE MACKENZIE OVER THERE?
SHE LOOKS REAL GOOD IN HER DESIGNER BIKINI.

YOU FEEL ME?
OH MY GOD!

UGLY COW
WHO DID THIS?

WHO DID THIS?

HEY! DON'T LOOK AT ME!
KENZ? WHAT'S GOING ON?

YOU TELL ME! IT WAS FINE WHEN I PUT IT IN MY LOCKER THIS MORNING.
YOU'RE THE ONLY ONE WHO KNOWS THE COMBINATION, TOINE!

HANG ON, WHAT!?! YOU THINK I DID IT?
WELL? DID YOU?

HOLD UP, GIRL, I DIDN'T EVEN—
DON'T YOU DARE START CALLING ME "GIRL" AGAIN.

I thought I had nothing left to lose. I was wrong.
WOMAN

shy_shelbi
Let's start simple
Go see sad, homely little Cody.

Tell her she deserves what she got.

She did it for nothing.
And she wasted my time.

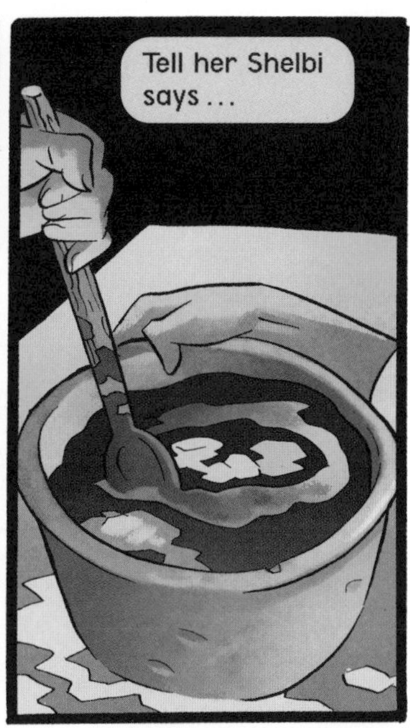
Tell her Shelbi says . . .

She's a lost cause.

A loser for life.

sigh
COOKIES AGAIN? I DREAM OF THE DAY YOU LEARN TO COOK DINNER.

CAN YOU AT LEAST CLEAN THIS UP? IT'S ALREADY 7:00.
TASTE THESE. I'M NOT SURE WHAT I DID WRONG.
WAY TO UPSELL, HON.

TASTES FINE TO ME.
THEY'RE JUST NOT . . . MAGIC. NOT LIKE SHE MADE THEM.

I DON'T UNDERSTAND. I FOLLOWED THE RECIPE LIKE ALWAYS.
HON, SOONER OR LATER YOU'RE GONNA HAVE TO ACCEPT IT'S POSSIBLE TO DO EVERYTHING RIGHT AND STILL FAIL.

IT'S THAT FRIEND OF YOURS, ISN'T IT? HAVE YOU GONE TO SEE HER IN THE HOSPITAL?
SHE WASN'T REALLY A FRIEND.

RIGHT, BECAUSE FAYE FAULKNER IS TOO TOUGH AND INDEPENDENT TO NEED FRIENDS.
SHE MADE FUN OF MY HAT.

THAT'S YOUR EXCUSE EVERY TIME.
I CAN'T HELP IT IF EVERYONE MAKES A BIG DEAL OUT OF IT.

YOU USE THAT HAT TO MEASURE PEOPLE, EXCEPT NO ONE MEASURES UP.

THAT'S NOT WHAT IT'S FOR! I TOLD YOU, IT'S SO I'LL ALWAYS REMEMBER HER.

AND ALL THE GOOD SHE DID, EVEN THOUGH NO ONE ELSE CARED.
I CARE.
ELVIRA WAS LONELY TOO, FAYE.

AND SHE WASN'T TOO PROUD TO BEFRIEND A CURIOUS LITTLE KID WHO THOUGHT WITCHES WERE SCARY.

MAYBE YOU SHOULD LEARN A LESSON FROM THAT.

JÚLIO? YOU OKAY? HAVE YOU SEEN HER?
ST. MARY'S HOSPITAL
EMERGENCY ENTRANCE
TRAUMA CENTER

I . . .
I DON'T KNOW WHAT TO SAY.
HAH! THAT'S A FIRST.

OH GOD! I WISH I DIDN'T EXIST!

CHILL OUT! OBVIOUSLY, CODY WOULDN'T AGREE.
SHE MUST HATE ME!

ALL RIGHT, DRAMA BOY. LET'S DIAL IT BACK A LITTLE. NOBODY HATES YOU.

YOU HAVE NO IDEA. YOU WOULDN'T BELIEVE ME . . .
ACTUALLY . . .

Kill yourself, loser.
. . . I'M PRETTY SURE I WOULD.

YOU'RE NOT THE ONLY ONE.
I . . . I COULDN'T TELL ANYBODY.

YOU DON'T KNOW WHAT IT'S LIKE TO FEEL THAT ALONE.
oh, C'MON! REMEMBER WHO YOU'RE TALKING TO?

AND YOU'RE NOT ALONE, OKAY?

FAYE?
HEY THERE. HOW ARE YOU HOLDING UP?

TRACTION. AT LEAST THERE'S INTERNET TV HERE. I CAN WATCH WHAT I WANT FOR A CHANGE.
YOU CAN CATCH UP ON THAT BAKING SHOW. SPEAKING OF WHICH . . .

I, err, BROUGHT YOU SOME COOKIES.
YOU MUST THINK I'M AN IDIOT.

TOLD YOU SO. STICKING YOUR NOSE IN OTHER PEOPLE'S BUSINESS? STUPID.
YOU KINDA BROUGHT THIS . . .
uh . . .

YEAH. I DON'T KNOW WHAT I WAS THINKING.
HEY!

I DO. MY OLD TEACHER, OL' LADY LEDOUX?

SHE'D HAVE LIKED YOU.

UMM . . . ERR . . .
I JUST WANTED TO COME SAY, UH . . .
. . . THANK YOU . . . AND STUFF . . .

AND HE EVEN BROUGHT FLOWERS. WHAT A GENTLEMAN.

YEAH, SORRY. I BOUGHT THEM A COUPLE DAYS AGO, AND I, uh, COULDN'T . . .
THEY'RE THE ONLY FLOWERS I'VE GOTTEN.
THANKS.

LET'S GET 'EM IN SOME FRESH WATER.
SO, uh, HOW'S . . . LIFE . . . ?

HAHAHAHAHAHAHAHA!
OH MY GOD I'M S-SORR—
HAHAHAHAHAHAHA!
OW!

ARE YOU OKAY?
OW! IT HURTS WHEN I LAUGH!
SORRY.

NO, I . . . *THANK YOU.* I *NEEDED* THAT.
IT FEELS LIKE *YEARS* SINCE I'VE LAUGHED ABOUT *ANYTHING.*

THERE, THAT OUGHT TO BRIGHTEN UP THE ROOM.
WHOA, ARE *THOSE MY* FLOWERS?

THEY JUST NEEDED A LITTLE *TLC.*
I GUESS FAYE'S GOT A *MAGIC TOUCH.*

THANKS FOR *COMING,* JÚLIO. IT'S *NICE* TO HAVE *COMPANY.*

IN THIS PLACE, I'M IN MY ELEMENT.
IN THIS CIRCLE, I AM IN MY POWER.
UNWOMAN
REVEAL THE HAND OF SHY SHELBI.
SHOW ME HOW FAR HER REACH EXTENDS.
SHOW ME EVERYONE SHE'S TOUCHED.

the shy_shelbi program

Step 5: Alphas Don't Run in Packs

The higher you climb, the more people will drag you down trying to ride your coattails. Cut them loose. It's lonely at the top, but the view is worth it. Step 5, there's only one first place. Make sure it's yours . . . more

THIS IS ABOUT SHY SHELBI. I KNOW EVERYTHING. ABOUT ALL OF YOU.

HANG ON, YOU'RE SHELBI?
THIS WHOLE THING IS JUST A BLACKMAIL SCHEME RUN BY A STUDENT?

BUT . . . I'M A TEACHER! I DON'T HAVE ANY MONEY!
HOW COULD YOU DO THIS TO ME?

I'M NOT SHY SHELBI, MR. KAUFMAN.

JÚLIO, TELL US WHAT SHELBI DID TO YOU.
I . . . uh . . .

C'MON. CAPTIVE AUDIENCE! DON'T TELL ME YOU HAVE STAGE FRIGHT.
IT'S NOT FUNNY.

I DIDN'T WANT TO HURT ANYONE.
BUT PEOPLE KEPT GETTING HURT AROUND ME, BECAUSE I WOULDN'T DO WHAT SHE TOLD ME TO. AND THEN . . .

THEN KURT REJECTED YOU FROM THE DRAMA CLUB.
HE SAID I WAS TOO . . . TOO MUCH DRAMA.

SHELBI TOLD ME I HAD TO. IT SEEMED LIKE THE LEAST HARM I COULD DO.
IT WASN'T.

I MEAN, I **KNOW** I'M . . . YOU KNOW. **EXTRA.** I JUST THOUGHT, IF **ANYONE** WOULD GET ME . . .
AFTER THAT, I THOUGHT I HAD **NOBODY.**
AND THEN ***CODY*** . . .

SHE SAW YOU IN ***TROUBLE.*** AND SHE WANTED TO ***HELP.*** NO MATTER THE COST.

SO WHO ***DID*** ALL THIS? WHO ***IS*** SHY SHELBI?
YOU WOULDN'T **BELIEVE** ME IF I ***TOLD*** YOU.

AT ***THIS*** POINT, I'D BELIEVE ***ANYTHING.***
NO. I HAVE TO ***SHOW*** YOU.

THEY CALL THIS THE LOSER TABLE BECAUSE THEY THINK IT'S AS FAR AS YOU CAN FALL. THE BOTTOM.
BUT THAT'S NOT WHAT IT IS. THIS IS THE PLACE WHERE WE CATCH EACH OTHER.
EVERYONE HOLD HANDS.

THIS ISN'T SOME KIND OF HIPPY-DIPPY HEALING THING, IS IT?
JUST DO ME A FAVOR, JÚLIO.

I WANT TO SHOW YOU SOMETHING.

A **CURSE** HANGS OVER THIS PLACE. BUT IN THIS **CIRCLE**, IT CAN'T HURT US.

BECAUSE IN THIS CIRCLE, WE ARE IN OUR **POWER**.
WE **SUMMON** YOU, CURSED ONE, BY THE NAME OF ***SHY SHELBI.***

DON'T BREAK THE *CIRCLE!*
WHAT THE *HELL!?*
WHAT *IS IT?!*
HOLY MOLY!

SHE'S WHAT I CALL A CURSE CREATURE. THIS ONE PREYS ON OUR LONELINESS, FEEDS ON OUR MISERY.
AND LIKE ALL SPIRITS, SHE'S NEVER SATISFIED.

SHE CHOSE US BECAUSE WE THOUGHT WE WERE ALONE.
BUT LOOK AROUND.

IT TURNS OUT, WE'RE ALL IN THIS TOGETHER.

WELL, SHELBI? GOT ANYTHING TO SAY?
LOSERS! JUST KILL YOURSELVES.

EXCUSE ME!?!
DON'T YOU SPEAK TO MR. KAUFMAN LIKE THAT! HE'S GOT A PHD! WE LOOK UP TO HIM!

YEAH! SCREW YOU, DUDE! I'M GONNA BE A STAR!
I'M A NICE PERSON, DAMMIT!
YEAH! YOU'RE THE UGLY ONE!

GO TO HELL! I'M . . . I'M NOT ASHAMED.

YOUR TRICKS DON'T WORK HERE. IN THIS CIRCLE, WE'RE IN OUR POWER.

SKRRREEEEEEEEEEEEEEEEEEE
BY YOUR OWN CURSE, I *BANISH* YOU!

BACK WHERE YOU **CAME** FROM. JUST ANOTHER **EMPTY INSULT,** ANOTHER SORRY ATTEMPT TO **TEAR US DOWN.**
LOSER
SOONER OR **LATER,** WE ALL LEARN TO **IGNORE** YOU.

IS THAT IT? ARE YOU LOSERS DONE WITH YOUR LITTLE GAME YET?
WHAT? YOU DIDN'T SEE THE DEMON THING FLOATING OVER THE TABLE?

SHE DIDN'T SEE ANYTHING. HER TYPE NEVER DOES.
I SAW A BUNCH OF DORKS PLAYING OUIJI WITHOUT A BOARD.
SO WHAT'S SHE EVEN DOING HERE?

GOOD QUESTION. I'M NOT PART OF YOUR LITTLE CLUB. IT'S NOT LIKE I EVER SAT AT THE LOSER TABLE.
BUT YOU LIVE IN FEAR OF IT, DON'T YOU?
WHATEVER. KEEP DREAMING, FREAK.

YOU THINK STANDING ABOVE EVERYONE MAKES YOU BETTER, KEEPS YOU FROM SINKING TO OUR LEVEL.

KEEPS YOU SAFE FROM BEING HURT, OR HEARTBROKEN, OR ASHAMED. BELIEVE ME, I GET IT.

THAT'S WHY YOU PLAYED SHELBI'S GAME.
TRASHED MY LOCKER. DESTROYED MACKENZIE'S LAPTOP. AND . . .
OTHER STUFF.

SEE, I KNOW ALL YOUR DIRTY SECRETS, DEARIE. SO YOU'RE DONE.
NO MORE PRANKS, OR I EXPOSE YOU.

YOU CAN'T PROVE ANYTHING!

UP TO YOU. BUT REMEMBER, YOU'VE GOT A LOT MORE TO LOSE THAN ME.

WE FEW, WE HAPPY FEW, WE BAND OF BROTHERS . . .
FOR HE TO-DAY THAT SHEDS HIS BLOOD WITH ME SHALL BE MY BROTHER—
- Faye's Journal, November 1st -

OR SISTER!
THAT'S JUST HOW IT WAS WRITTEN, STEF.
AND GENTLEMEN IN ENGLAND NOW A-BED SHALL THINK THEMSELVES ACCURSED THEY WERE NOT HERE . . .

I'd gotten so used to it, so used to having no one . . .
AND HOLD THEIR MANHOODS CHEAP WHILST ANY SPEAKS THAT FOUGHT WITH US . . .
WELL, IF YOU GUYS WANT TO STAGE THIS, WE NEED TO DISCUSS SOME THINGS.
HE'S NOT BAD, THOUGH. SMUG LITTLE TWERP.

...I guess I never realized how cold I was.
GET WELL FUND
Coming out of the cold can be just as scary and painful as going into it.
In a way it's worse. Knowing how it feels to lose everything...
SWEET RIDE.
RAFFI, RIGHT?
THANKS. YOU GUYS NEED A LIFT?
hmph!
...it felt safer to have nothing.
KAUFMAN? WHAT'S GOING ON?

JUST TIRED OF LOOKING AT THE DAMN THING.
YOU GOT THE BOARD'S PERMISSION?
NOPE.

But I think maybe being scared is better than being numb.
YA KNOW SOMETHING, GRETCHEN? I THINK I CAN LIVE WITH THIS.

THANKS FOR COMING IN, MRS. FAULKNER. I'M AFRAID A TROUBLING MATTER HAS BEEN BROUGHT TO OUR ATTENTION.

WE'VE BEEN INFORMED THAT YOUR DAUGHTER MAY BE RESPONSIBLE FOR THIS "SHY SHELBI" CYBER-BULLYING INCIDENT.
HANG IN THER
ARE YOU KIDDING ME? I'M THE ONE WHO—
THIS IS THE FIRST I'VE HEARD OF ANY OF THIS!

PERHAPS IF YOU WERE MORE INVOLVED WITH FAYE'S LIFE—
HANG ON! DO YOU HAVE ANY EVIDENCE?

ANOTHER STUDENT CAME FORWARD.
SO IT'S THEIR WORD AGAINST FAYE'S?!

IT'S NOT THAT SIMPLE. WE TAKE BULLYING VERY SERIOUSLY, MRS. FAULKNER.

THE MATTER IS UNDER INVESTIGATION, BUT THE SCHOOL BOARD HAS VOTED THAT FAYE BE REMOVED.
I SEE.

JUST TILL WE GET TO THE BOTTOM OF ALL THIS.
AND I CAN GUESS WHERE ARGUING WITH THEM WILL GET ME.

GHTIN' SPIRIT!
GOING SOMEWHERE, FAULKNER?

IT WAS YOU, huh? THIS IS MY SHOCKED FACE.
MY DAD HAS A LOTTA PULL ON THE SCHOOL BOARD.
SO I GUESS I'LL SEE YOU AROUND. OR MAYBE NOT.

IT'S FOR THE BEST, I SUPPOSE. A SCAPEGOAT MEANS SHY SHELBI LOSES ANY LINGERING MYSTIQUE. ONE MORE NAIL IN HER COFFIN.

BUT HERE'S THE THING ABOUT CALLING SOMEONE'S BLUFF, BRYCE.
SLAM

YOU BETTER BE DAMN SURE THEY'RE BLUFFING.
EXIT

THAT'S GREAT NEWS. I'M GLAD WE COULD COME TO A MUTUALLY BENEFICIAL ARRANGEMENT.
I THINK YOU'LL FIND I'M A GOOD FRIEND TO HAVE, MR. ATLEY.
CONGRATULATIONS, BUTTERCUP. YOU'RE GOING TO HARVARD.
YOU'RE THE BEST DAD IN THE WORLD!

DON'T GET UP, MOM. I'LL GET IT.
KNOCK KNOCK

MISS SPOONER? I NEED TO SPEAK TO YOUR PARENTS.

WOW! CHECK OUT MISS POPULARITY.
ST. MARY'S HOSPITAL

HAVEN'T SEEN YOU IN A WHILE.
I WAS BUSY SORTING OUT OUR LITTLE PROBLEM.
THAT'S NOT THE ONLY THING YOU SORTED OUT.

YOU MEAN BRYCE? THEY FOUND THE CLIPPERS?
HOW DID YOU KNOW WHERE THEY WERE?
TAMMY
OxHORN

WITCHCRAFT, OF COURSE. BUT I NEEDN'T HAVE BOTHERED.
ONLY BRYCE IS ARROGANT ENOUGH TO PUT THEM BACK IN THE TOOL DRAWER ALL COVERED IN FINGERPRINTS AND BRAKE FLUID.

I WISH YOU'D JUST LEFT IT ALONE. NOW WE ALL HAVE TO LIVE WITH KNOWING . . .

KNOWING SHE'S THE ONE WHO PUT YOUR MOM IN THE HOSPITAL?
WOULD YOU RATHER SHE GET AWAY WITH IT? MAYBE DO SOMETHING EVEN WORSE NEXT TIME?

SHE SAYS SHE DIDN'T MEAN IT TO BE THAT BAD. SHE THOUGHT IT WOULD JUST BE A FENDER BENDER.
AND THAT MAKES IT OKAY?
YOU DON'T UNDERSTAND!

THE POLICE TOOK HER AWAY IN HANDCUFFS.
I'LL SUE THE DEPARTMENT!
I NEED YOU TO CALM DOWN, MR. SPOONER.
MOM! TELL THEM I DIDN'T MEAN IT!

TELL THEM IT'S OKAY!
I . . . uh . . . IT'S NOT.
DON'T WORRY, BUTTERCUP.

DAD TOOK HER SIDE, OF COURSE.
DADDY WILL TAKE CARE OF THIS.

MOM WON'T TALK TO BRYCE. OR DAD. I THINK THEY'RE GONNA GET A DIVORCE.

I CAN'T TALK HER OUT OF IT.
HEY! IT'S NOT MY FAULT YOUR SISTER'S A SOCIOPATH!

YOU KEEP LOOKING FOR A WAY TO MAKE EVERYBODY HAPPY! BUT SOME PEOPLE ARE ONLY HAPPY WHEN THEY'RE MAKING EVERYONE ELSE MISERABLE!
YOU COULD AT LEAST HAVE CHECKED WITH ME BEFORE YOU BLEW MY FAMILY APART!

YA KNOW WHAT!?

sigh
NEVER MIND.

THIS IS WHY I NEVER LEFT THE LOSER TABLE, AND NEVER KEPT UP WITH ANYONE WHO DID.
THIS IS WHY I DON'T STICK MY NOSE IN OTHER PEOPLE'S BUSINESS. WITCHES AREN'T GOOD AT . . .
sigh

I'M . . .
. . . NOT GOOD AT BEING FRIENDS.
I SAY THINGS PEOPLE DON'T LIKE TO HEAR. I DIG THINGS UP PEOPLE WANT TO KEEP BURIED. I TRY NOT TO, BUT . . .

SOONER OR LATER, EVERYONE ENDS UP HATING ME.

I DIDN'T MEAN TO MESS THINGS UP FOR YOU, CODY. I WAS JUST TRYING TO HELP.

SORRY.
FAYE, WAIT!

I . . . I NEVER THANKED YOU.

YOU'RE THE BEST FRIEND I EVER HAD. AND I DON'T KNOW WHY YOU EVEN BOTHERED HELPING ME.

BUT IF YOU HADN'T, I DON'T KNOW WHAT MIGHT HAVE HAPPENED.
I'LL NEVER FORGET WHAT YOU DID. I OWE YOU MORE THAN I COULD EVER REPAY.
YOU DON'T OWE ME ANYTHING, CODY.
REALLY.

SHUT UP AND **LISTEN!**
MY **MOTHER** DEVOTED HER **WHOLE LIFE** TO MY DAD, MY SISTER, AND **ME**. SHE NEVER ASKED FOR **ANYTHING.**
LOOK WHERE **THAT** GOT HER.

TURNS OUT, IF YOU SPEND YOUR LIFE HELPING **OTHER PEOPLE** AND ASK **NOTHING** IN **RETURN** . . .
. . . YOU'LL END UP WITH **NOTHING.**

I DON'T **HAVE** ANY WAY TO **REPAY** YOU. BUT **SOMEONE** WILL.
SOMEONE WHO **NEEDS** YOU LIKE **I** DID.

SO I THOUGHT, WHAT DOES A **WITCH FOR HIRE** NEED TO **KICK-START** HER **CAREER?**
MY **CAREER?**

YOU'RE A **BIG DEAL,** FAYE FAULKNER. KNOW YOUR **WORTH.**

Thanks to Charlotte, Kay, and everyone at Abrams
for believing in this project.

Thanks to Scott Zoback for having my back and
Alan Spiegel for being a warm, friendly presence
at Comic Cons since forever. You guys are the best.

Thanks to Paget, Azmeer, Anne-Claude, and everyone
else who let me talk their ear off about this project.
Sometimes you just need to hear the ideas out loud
and good feedback is priceless.

Thanks to Jessica and Brian Berlin, Melanie,
Barbara, Jen, Lesley, and all my beloved community
for moral, emotional, and spiritual support.

Thanks Mom and Dad for always believing in my work.

As ever, thanks to Kelly Crumrin.